God's Whispers

Ruth McDonald Mair

Editor: Tracy Ruckman

Illustrator: Valerie Bouthyette.

ISBN: 978-1-60383-433-9

Published by:
Holy Fire Publishing
PO Box 1886
DeLand, FL 32721

www.ChristianPublish.com

Printed in the United States of America and the United Kingdom

Dedication

This book is dedicated to my parents, Walter and Lethie McDonald.

Without them I may have grown up not ever knowing how wonderful God truly is.

Thank you, Mama and Daddy, for teaching me how to hear God's beautiful whispers.

Seth was helping with Sunday dinner preparations by setting the table. "Mom, my Sunday School teacher says that God whispers to each of us every day and that we just have to listen to hear it. Is that true?"

His mom set the bowl of green beans on the table and said, "Yes, I believe you can hear God whisper to you."

"But I've never heard God whisper before. I've heard my friends whisper at school during class and I've heard you and daddy whisper about Christmas and birthday presents, but I've never heard God whisper. Why not?"

Seth's mom sat down in a chair and motioned him to her.

Seth walked over and climbed into his mom's lap. She wrapped her arms around him in a big bear hug and said, "God just whispered to you. Did you hear it?"

"I didn't hear anything."

"I think you just need to listen in a different way. We don't always hear God's whispers with our ears."

"Our ears are what we hear with and I didn't hear anything."

Seth's mom smiled at him. "God just whispered to you again. God's whispers aren't always loud enough to hear them with our ears. Sometimes we have to feel them or see them. When I hugged you that was a whisper from God telling you how much you are loved. When I smiled at you that was a whisper from God telling you how special you are."

"Wow!" said Seth. "I've never thought about being able to hear a whisper that way."

All during dinner, Seth continued thinking about what his mom had said. When he and his older sister finished washing and drying the dishes, he asked his mom if he could go outside. She told him that he could, but not to go too far because they were going to be leaving for grandma and grandpa's house in a little while.

Seth went outside and patted his dog, Wesley, on the head. Wesley wagged his tail and took off running ahead of Seth. They ran to the edge of the shallow creek that ran behind Seth's house and sat down on a large rock. Seth listened to the sound of the creek flowing over the rocks for a few minutes. The summer sun was beating down on him and Wesley, so they moved into the shade of the large oak tree that grew by the creek. In the shade, Seth enjoyed the light breeze that was blowing and as they cooled off, Wesley rolled in the grass. Wesley stretched out and decided this was a good place for a quick nap. Wildflowers grew all around them. As Seth looked at one, a beautiful huge Monarch butterfly landed on it. Seth watched until it fluttered away in the breeze, off to another flower. Just then, a robin came swooping down out of the tree, landing on the ground not too far from Seth and Wesley.

Seth watched the robin hop along the ground. Soon it spied a worm and plucked it from the ground with its beak then immediately flew back up into the oak tree. Seth noticed the nest full of baby robins gobbling up worm.

"Seth!" called his mom. It was time to get ready for the trip to grandma and grandpa's house.

Seth always liked going to visit his grandparents. Grandma always had fresh baked cookies and a tall glass of cold milk ready for him when he got there. It was a short ride to his grandparents', but on the way, it got cloudy and started to rain.

"Great," thought Seth, "Because of the rain, I won't be able to go out and play in the fort that Grandpa built for me." But by the time Seth and his family arrived, the rain had almost stopped. As they got out of the car, Seth looked up and saw a huge rainbow going across the sky. "Look at that rainbow!" He pointed to colorful arc.

"That is beautiful," his mother patted his shoulder.

Seth's dad said, "You know Seth, the rainbow is God's way of letting us know that he will always love and care for us and never destroy the world again with a flood the way he did when he asked Noah to build the ark."

As they headed inside, Seth's grandma was setting a huge plate of freshly baked chocolate chip cookies and large glass of cold milk on the table. "Here you go, Seth. I made a snack just for you. I know a growing boy like you needs to have snacks." Seth gave his grandma and grandpa a big hug and sat down at the table to enjoy the snack his grandma had prepared for him. When he finished his cookies and milk, he went out to play in the fort until it was time to go home.

On the way home, Seth's mom turned to him and asked, "Seth, have you thought anymore about trying to listen for God's whispers?"

Seth got a large smile on his face and said, "Mom, I heard lots of whispers from God today."

"You did? What did He say to you?"

"Well, when I went outside to play after dinner, Wesley met me at the door and when I patted his head, he wagged his tail a whole bunch. I think that was God's way of telling me that Wesley loves me and protects me. Then, when we went to the creek, I could hear the water running over the rocks and I realized that was God's whisper reminding me that if I believe in Him, He will take me to heaven when I die."

Seth's mom and dad looked at each other and smiled. "What else did you hear today, Seth?" asked Seth's dad.

"Oh. Wesley and me were sitting on a rock by the creek and it got too warm so we moved into the shade and there was a nice breeze blowing that cooled us off. That was probably God saying that he'll keep me warm on cold winter days and cool me off in the summer. Then, there was a butterfly getting some nectar from one of the wildflowers and a robin that came down out of the tree and got a worm to take back to its nest of babies. I thought I heard God say that he will provide food for me and not let me go hungry."

"Anything else?" Seth's mom asked.

"Well, on the way to Grandma and Grandpa's it started to rain and I was really disappointed thinking that I wouldn't be able to play out in the fort because of the rain. But then when we got there, it had almost quit raining and we saw that rainbow in the sky. I decided that was God telling me that just because something comes up that we aren't expecting, things will always work out in the end."

"You listened very well, Seth." His dad gave him a "thumbs-up."

"I heard one more thing today. When Grandma gave me the cookies she had made and the big glass of milk, I heard God say that my family loves me and will always be there for me and that He is part of my family."

His mom nodded. "You heard a lot of whispers from God today. I am so glad you figured out how to hear them."

Seth smiled. "I learned that God really does whisper to us every day, we just have to learn to listen with not just our ears, but listen with our heart, too."

CPSIA information can be obtained
at www.ICGtesting.com
Printed in the USA
LVIC04n0919081216
516321LV00002B/2

* 9 7 8 1 6 0 3 8 3 4 3 3 9 *